Feral Spirits

Feral Spirits

Iridescent Toad Publishing

Iridescent Toad Publishing.

Book cover design by BRoseDesignz.

First edition. ISBN: 978-1-913779-07-8

*Extra special thanks to Alysha Thornton
for helping me bring this book to life.*

Feral Spirits

Chapter One

"Rainbow! Get your arse over here!"

Raine cringed and turned around to see who had a death wish. The only thing she hated more than being a shapeshifter was hearing her full name. Rainbow. She didn't know what drugs her mother had been on when she had chosen that name, but was sure that there had probably been at least some weed involved. Knowing what her mother was like, there had probably been far more than that in her system.

"What do you want?" Raine asked as she jogged over to Lucas.

He frowned as he looked at her.

"Are you not going to the pack meeting tonight?" he asked. "Jenna said that you're going to skip it to go and hang out with that *human*."

Raine crossed her arms, raising one eyebrow. Lucas said the word human as if it left a horrible taste in his mouth.

"Do you have a problem with my girlfriend?" she demanded.

"You know the rules," he replied. "You can't settle down with a human – not for a long-term relationship anyway. She will die decades before you do. Besides, what would happen when you start being mistaken for her daughter? And then her granddaughter? It's not right."

Raine threw her hands up in the air before they fell back to her side.

"Are you fucking kidding me?" she retorted. "I have only been seeing Denny for a couple of months. We are far from talking about what I am and what that means."

Lucas sighed and ran a hand through his short red hair. Wrinkles creased on his forehead as he frowned at Raine.

"You know that either way it will never work out. The humans don't give a shit about us. Hell, you have heard all of the stories about them hunting us. What makes you think that this one girl is worth it? Would you really give the cold shoulder to your family over her?"

Raine growled at Lucas, the hair on her arms standing on end as she bared her teeth. He stepped back, amusement sparkling in his eyes though. Raine watched as his lips twitched and she knew that whatever was about to leave his mouth next wouldn't be nice.

Instead of fighting with the pack leader, she turned around and walked away. She knew that he could call her back and insist on her going to the meeting, but she also knew that he wouldn't. Although Lucas was the leader of the shapeshifter pack, he never forced any of its members to do something that they didn't want to. He was the kind of leader who believed that everybody still had free will; that they were better than their more animalistic side.

Raine wasn't so sure of that though. She looked at the blood beneath her fingernails and shivered. *I am not a good person.* With a shake of her head, she stuffed her hands back into her pockets. There was no more time to think about that. Denny would be waiting for her. A smile spread across her face as she entered the pack house and headed off towards her room, thinking about sweet Denny.

Denny would be the first to insist that she was

anything but sweet. Raine was sure of it. Denny was loud and outspoken. It had come from years of working as a mechanic and being surrounded by men. She'd had to fight to prove herself every day. And prove it she did. It was one of the things that Raine had first noticed about her. The woman was not afraid of anything. She was the complete opposite of Raine.

Raine entered her room and slammed the door shut, twisting the lock into place. She could hear shouting in the halls as she disappeared into her bathroom and started scrubbing away at the blood and the dirt that clung to her like a second skin. Once she was showered, she picked out a pair of ripped jeans and a black tank top. It was simple but it was enough. Denny would be taking her to the history museum that had just opened.

She looked in the mirror and tugged at the hem of her top. *Are you sure this is ok?* a little voice in the back of her mind whispered. *Denny is used to dating women who get dressed up for dates.*

Raine tried to shake the thoughts from her mind as she walked downstairs and then outside to the rough-looking truck that was waiting for her. She couldn't win though. The thoughts danced around in her mind even as Denny bent forward to give her a quick kiss.

Chapter Two

"So, who's that paranoid-looking redhead who was watching me?" Denny asked. "It's like he thought I was about to invade the house and murder somebody."

Raine cringed. She still hadn't figured out a good way to explain the pack house to Denny. She didn't want to lie to her girlfriend, but protecting the pack was always the priority. It had to be. The pack was the only family she'd ever known and she couldn't afford to put them in danger – especially in view of what had happened to another pack before. One person had let their guard down and revealed their true identity to a human. The human had freaked out over it and every shapeshifter in the pack was hunted for sport until they were all eradicated. Upon hearing of it, Raine had sobbed until she was sick.

"Earth to Rainbow."

"Fuck off," Raine muttered as she looked at Denny.

"You know I hate that."

"You disappeared into your head again. I've been saying your name for the past five minutes. What's going on with you tonight?"

Raine sighed and shrugged. She fidgeted with the single ring on her right index finger.

"I don't know," she said. "There's just some stuff going on in my family and things are a little bit tense at the moment."

"What kind of things?"

A looming war.

"Just some personal stuff," Raine said with a shrug. "We're supposed to be having fun. I don't want to ruin our date."

Denny grinned and reached over to take Raine's hand in hers. She brought it to her lips and placed a kiss on the back of it.

"You know you can tell me anything," she said kindly. "I'm not going to judge you. Whatever it is, we are in it together."

Raine nodded, a lump rising in her throat. She

hated that she had to lie to Denny, but she felt that it was the only option. Revealing her true identity could mean death. She simply wasn't willing to take the risk – especially because she was already unsure of why Denny chose to be with her.

How could I possibly tell my girlfriend that I can turn into a panther? There should be a book written about it, Raine thought to herself. She stared out of the truck window at the town passing them by. Everybody was free to live as they wanted; to *be* with who they wanted. Not her though. She was one person with the pack and another person entirely with everyone else in her life. She had to be. Of course, the "everyone else" in her life extended exclusively to Denny. There was nobody else. The pack didn't feel like real family to Raine. Even though she had been with them longer than anybody else in her life, they only existed to keep each other alive. Safety in numbers, the pack mentality liked to claim. Over time though, she had started to think that it was all bullshit.

The truck pulled off the road and Denny shut the engine off. She twisted in her seat to look at Raine.

"Earth to Raine," she said. "I think I lost you again… Ok, enough of this. What's going on? I know it's not unusual for you to be distant sometimes but this is another level entirely. Is there somewhere else you'd rather be, or perhaps someone else that you'd rather be with?"

"There is nobody else I would rather be with."

Raine's cheeks turned crimson as she squeezed Denny's hand tightly. Denny frowned and pulled her hand back.

"Then stop shutting me out like this," Denny insisted. "I really like you but I'm not going to be your second choice."

Raine squirmed, embarrassed and frustrated. She was already making a mess of her relationship. She wanted it to go well but it seemed like nothing had been going the way she wanted it to lately.

"I'm just going through some things with my family and I don't want to scare you away," she said.

"Look, I get that," Denny said with a sigh as she combed her hand through her dark hair. "I'm not here to waste my time though. I thought you knew that."

Raine's bottom lip trembled. She had to work hard to keep the emotion out of her voice.

"Well, if you think I'm wasting your time then maybe I should just leave."

Before Denny had a chance to answer, Raine opened the truck door and got out. She slammed it behind her and stormed off into the woods that lined the edge of the road. She didn't want to sit there and argue with Denny. It would only end badly. She could already feel herself losing control of the panther. Her hands were shaking and she could feel the hair on her arms standing on end. If she hadn't left the truck when she did, Denny would be trapped in there with an angry animal.

Raine shook her head as the tips of her fangs started to poke her bottom lip. She ran her tongue across them as she darted deeper into the woods. She kept running until she could no longer hear Denny calling after her. Finally, she could give in to the panther.

Chapter Three

Shapeshifting had never been easy for anybody. The worst part was the feeling of bones breaking; thousands of times over before stitching themselves back together in a new formation. Not only that, but organs would rearrange themselves in the human body in order to fit into the form of the person's animal. Sometimes, a shifter's body would compress if their animal form was smaller than their human one. For Raine, her human body would expand when she shifted into her panther form. She had always disliked the process.

She was crouched down, shaking in the mud, her chest heaving. She had changed but it had come at a cost. It had made her feel weak. She had always struggled with the shift, and more so than the other pack members. It was a fact that none of them had tried to hide from her. Although their shifts were painful, their ability to recover from them was much faster. Whenever she shifted, she would feel sick for days afterwards. There was something about it that had never felt natural.

Of course it doesn't feel natural, you dumb arse, Raine thought as she steadied herself on her paws. She flexed them, feeling the soft mud between her toes. Her ears twitched as she listened to the sounds of the woods around her. In the distance, she could still hear Denny calling her name. Denny's stubbornness was a trait that Raine both adored and hated. Denny had no boundaries. She was open in a way that Raine only wished she could be.

Raine looked back towards the direction of the truck. If she wanted to, she could shift back and go to Denny for another difficult conversation. Alternatively, she could continue on to the pack house and attend the meeting there, pretending once more that she felt like she was one of them.

It was an easy decision to make.

****

Although the pack house could be described as many things, it could never be described as quiet. That would be impossible. There were too many people living under one roof for it to ever be completely silent. Raine stood inside a tiny shed at the edge of the pack's outdoor territory. She grabbed the small plastic storage box with her name on it and pulled out a fresh set of clothing.

Any member of a pack was long past caring about being naked in front of others. It was simply something that was unavoidable. Human clothes would always split and fall off during a shapeshift.

Once she had changed into a new set of human clothes, Raine entered the pack house via the back door. She quickly realised that she was walking into complete chaos. From the meeting room on the other side of the house, she could hear shouting. It didn't surprise her that things weren't going well. Within the pack, that was often the case.

She sighed and walked through the empty halls to join the pack and find out what was going on. That way, she wouldn't have to swallow her pride later to ask Lucas what had happened. He would never let her live it down.

The meeting room was filled just with pack members over the age of eighteen. All of them were talking amongst themselves. *Good*, Raine thought. *I should be able to slip into a seat in the back corner without being noticed.*

"Rainbow," Lucas announced at full volume for everyone in the room to hear. "I'm glad to see that you've finally decided to join us. To what do we owe this honour? Did you finally get tired of your little human pet?"

He was stood on top of the table in the centre of the room, commanding the pack's attention. Raine's cheeks flamed and her eyes watered as she slumped down further into her seat. With a triumphant smile, Lucas nodded at her. She hated that nod. They both knew he was right. It would never work out with Denny because she was a human.

Raine sighed and wiped away the tears that had started to slowly descend down her cheeks. She was on her own and she always had been. It was time to start accepting that. There would be no changing that fact. Although she hadn't broken up with Denny – at least not yet – the way she had taken off and left her alone in the truck like that had felt so final.

"So, Raine has finished entertaining her fantasies with a human," Lucas said as he raised his hands to command the room. "Good. We've got more important matters to discuss: like what has been killing the locals."

The pack had stopped talking. Raine cringed, wishing that she could disappear entirely. She had killed a hunter before but he had been ready to kill her first. It had been self-defence and Lucas knew it. Any human who found out about the pack had to be killed. Reports of a panther wandering around in the woods would make it more than a little obvious that something was amiss.

"There are reports that humans have been going missing from their beds in the middle of the night," Lucas continued. "At first the police thought it was someone from outside the town. However, when no ransom calls came in, they started to change their line of thinking and indeed, their approach towards the investigation."

He stepped back as his mate stepped forwards. Shelly was beautiful but she was as half-witted as the day was long. Raine rolled her eyes and stared out of the window at the dark night. Shelly's connection to the police would be the only thing to make her useful in this. Everything else about her was vapid and vain.

"The police have started searching through the woods for the dead children," she said. "About a week ago, a number of adults went missing too. It seems that whoever is doing this is completely ruthless. Anyway, two nights ago, the police found giant scratch marks on the bed frame of a woman who is still missing."

Shelly spoke as if seated around a campfire and telling spooky stories. She didn't sound like someone keen to inform the pack of the risk to their safety. Raine rolled her eyes and looked around. Lucas was nowhere to be seen. Sitting up a little straighter, Raine tried to listen out for him but she couldn't hear anything above the noise that Shelly was making.

Out of the window, Raine suddenly noticed a set of headlights. They beamed through into the room. Butterflies beat their wings relentlessly in her stomach as a familiar silhouette stood in stark contrast to the glow of light. Raine could only watch as Lucas approached the truck. She saw the subtle shift in his shoulders and the way he cracked his neck from one side to the other.

"*Fuck*," she said under her breath.

She dashed through the crowd of shapeshifters – who were now gathering by the window to see what was happening outside. Although she ran through the halls faster than any human could, it still wasn't enough. By the time she'd managed to get outside, Lucas was already talking to Denny. She moved to stand in between the pair. Denny didn't look pleased to see her.

She's still mad at me, Raine thought as she forced herself to smile whilst casually shoving Lucas out of the way.

"Who's this?" Denny asked as she gestured towards Lucas. "I thought you were living with some friends or something like that. Is that even true?"

"Yeah Rainbow," Lucas chided. "What am I to you? Who am I really?"

"Shut the hell up," Denny snapped at Lucas. "I'm talking to her, not you."

Lucas crossed his arms, the muscles in his biceps bulging.

"That's funny," he said. "People who stop by here usually have to speak to me first. All the same, I find you incredibly nosey and doubt that you have any reason to be here. Get off of my property or I'll call the police."

Denny's mouth dropped open as the blush in Raine's cheeks deepened. Raine couldn't believe what Lucas was saying. She knew that he didn't like humans anywhere near him. She knew that he could be ultra difficult at times but he was never like this with strangers. Instead, he was usually charming and sweet. Little old ladies loved him.

"What the hell are you doing?" Raine asked Lucas, almost growling at him.

"You came back home looking more upset than you have in a very long time," he replied. "Hell, I don't know if I have ever seen you come home looking like that before. I will be damned if she is going to show up at our home and make you feel that way again."

Raine shook her head and pointed a finger back towards the house.

"I can handle this, Lucas," she said. "Go inside."

Seeing that Lucas wasn't about to leave, she sighed.

"Please," she said, softer this time. "Leave us alone for a few minutes. I promise I won't be long."

After a few more moments of staring at Denny, Lucas nodded. He cracked his knuckles as he walked away. Once he was inside the house, Raine could still feel his eyes on her. She knew that just like the other shifters, he would be watching from the window.

Raine sighed and looked at Denny. Although she'd closed her mouth, it looked as if her eyes were about to bulge out of her head. It would be funny, if Denny wasn't still fuming.

"What the hell was that back there?" Denny demanded, her voice becoming louder with each word. "You just got out of the truck and left me. What kind of mature adult even does that? Seriously! We were just having a disagreement."

"Why are you here?"

Denny threw her hands up in the air, clearly exasperated.

"What do you mean? Of course I'm here," she said. "You took off into the woods and you looked deeply upset. What kind of person would I be if I didn't come looking for you? Are you actually kidding me right now?"

"We haven't been together that long," said Raine. "You have no reason to come looking for me. It was just an argument and you are far better off without me. Trust me on this."

Denny took a couple of steps towards Raine, closing the distance between them.

"How do you know that I'm better off without you? I've told you before that I'm looking forward to getting to know more about you, and that hasn't changed."

"And what if that isn't what I want?" Raine asked stubbornly. "What if I'd prefer to be left alone in my own misery?"

Denny laughed and shook her head, stepping in even closer. Her hands came up to cup either side of Raine's face.

"You are so beautiful, Raine. I think you're crazy, and a little stupid and naive. But you're so damn beautiful."

Raine squirmed away.

"Why are you trying so hard to make this work?" she insisted. "We should quit while we're ahead; end it now before it gets to be too much, and before we've had a chance to become too attached."

Denny scowled and took another step forwards until she was just inches away from Raine. Raine's breath caught in her throat as her heart pounded relentlessly. Denny cupped the back of Raine's head and pulled her in for a deep kiss.

"Too fucking late," Denny whispered.

Chapter Four

Denny had finally left, but only after Raine had agreed to a date with her for the following night. Raine walked back into the meeting room. She blushed as everyone turned to look at her.

"What the hell was that?" Lucas demanded.

Everyone was waiting for an answer that Raine had no desire to share. Her blush grew darker as she kept her mouth shut. She sat back down in the corner of the room. Lucas waited for a few moments longer until finally, he got back on top of the conference table.

The shapeshifters gathered around as files were handed out. Upon receiving one, Raine opened it reluctantly. There was a photograph of the bed that belonged to the last kidnapping victim. On the floor beside the bed, there were deeply carved claw marks – those that could only belong to a beast. Next to that photo, there was one of the woman who had gone missing. She looked a bit like

Denny; with dark hair, an angular nose, piercing eyes and a soft smile. Raine froze in her seat as she stared at the picture. Another night, it could be Denny.

"We know that a shapeshifter is behind this," Lucas explained. "We have no intelligence on who it could be though. There are numerous suspects."

He pointed at a screen as pictures of criminal shifters were projected onto it.

A female voice belonging to the woman to Raine's left spoke up. It was Dominique.

"What makes you think that all the suspects have been identified?" she asked. "This could just as easily be a new shifter on the scene – someone who is looking to prove themselves. What is there – in terms of evidence – to support the idea that the shifter behind this is known to us?"

"Look," said Lucas, sighing and folding his arms. "We have received detailed reports from the police about what they think the rogue shifter might look like."

"How can you be so sure with such little evidence? Besides, no live victims have been recovered," Dominique said. "You're allowing our pack to put themselves at the risk of trusting any other shifter who hasn't yet been listed as a suspect. How can you possibly know that every suspect has been identified? The simple answer is that you can't."

"Enough!" Lucas roared, tawny fur beginning to sprout from his skin.

Dominique got up from her seat and joined Lucas on top of the table. Raine cowered back in her seat, trying to make herself as small as possible. When the shifters started arguing like this, it usually meant that a fight was about to happen. Rarely was the leader of the pack ever involved though. The reason for this was simple: to challenge the pack leader, would mean a fight to the death.

Dominique knew this. She'd been warned of it the moment she arrived at the boundaries of the pack – having escaped from the troubles of her last one. Now, she was challenging the one person who had taken her in; the one person who had agreed to protect her and keep her safe.

Raine didn't know whether Dominique was stupid or harbouring a death wish. Knowing Dominique though, it was probably neither of those things. The woman was smart. She wouldn't present a challenge without planning to see it through. There was something else going on here; something that could easily result in the death of more than one member of the pack.

"What are you doing?" Shelly hissed as she grabbed Dominique's arm. "Sit the hell down before he loses it."

Dominique brushed Shelly's hand away. She wasn't interested in having anyone try to protect her. She was willing to make a challenge that she would not be able to back down from.

The entire meeting room was silent as the shifters watched the scene unfolding before them. Lucas stood tall, his nostrils flaring as he tried to remain in control. The last thing the pack needed was an angry lion going for throats.

His muscles tensed as he looked at Dominique and nodded.

"Ok," he said. "You and I both know what you are after. Either say it or back down. I warn you though, I will beat you and you will die. That peaceful life you were looking for? The one you wanted where a family existed? You do this and there will be none of that. Even if by some miracle you manage to beat me, there will be no warm and open arms. The pack will hate you. They will only follow you because you have beaten me, not because you are the leader that they need."

Feathers sprouted from Dominique's skin. Raine watched in horror as the bones along the woman's nose began to break, arranging themselves into a beak. Impressively, although Dominique would clearly be in pain from this, she didn't flinch. If anything, she stood taller. She was not going to bow before any man and for that, Raine admired her to a degree, wishing that she could be as strong – as both a shapeshifter and as a woman. Instead, she was the kind who backed down from a fight, hating who and what she was.

"You know, Lucas," said Dominique. "If that thought worried me, then I wouldn't be willing to challenge you. But, as it stands, I seem to be the only one willing to confront you for what you are turning the pack into. The others can see it but none of them dare to say anything."

"Make your challenge official or get off of pack territory," Lucas said, snarling.

Dominique smiled.

"I, Dominique Smith, challenge you, Lucas Warren."

Lucas nodded, long fangs protruding from his

mouth.

"The challenge has been issued," he said. "The battle will take place on Friday night, when the next snow falls."

Murmurs flew around the room as Dominique hopped down from the table and headed off to leave.

"I hope you're ready to die," she called back over her shoulder.

Chapter Five

Raine sat beside Denny in the truck. The air was chilly so they were huddled together beneath a blanket, perfectly cosy for their date at the drive-in. Raine had given up on the lame horror movie more than an hour ago. Instead, she was reading a book while Denny continued to watch the screen. Every now and then, Raine looked up from her book at her girlfriend and smiled. They were different to each other in so many ways and yet they clicked together like the pieces of a puzzle.

"What are you looking at?" Denny asked, looking at Raine with a soft smile.

"You."

"You are so damn beautiful," said Denny.

She put her hand up to cup Raine's cheek for a moment. Raine blushed and shook her head, allowing her hair to fall like a curtain in front of her face. Denny brushed it back in an instant, staring emotionally at Raine.

"Don't you ever try to hide how beautiful you are."

Raine's blush grew deeper as she tried to avoid Denny's gaze. It was too intense. The feelings between them were growing and they only had a few more days before the current state of Raine's life could change forever. Raine wouldn't be allowed to see Denny again if Dominique won the fight. Dominique hated humans more than she hated what Lucas was doing to the pack. Raine and Denny's relationship would have to come to an end. Whilst Lucas didn't approve of it and he voiced his opinion often, he had been very relaxed about the whole thing compared to what Dominique's approach would be.

Raine's stomach twisted as she glanced back at Denny. The smile had fallen from her face.

"We aren't going to have a repeat of what happened last night, are we?" Denny asked. "This hot and cold game is getting old really fast. Are you in this, or aren't you?"

"Of course I'm in this," Raine said defiantly. "That's not what's bothering me."

"Well, what is?" Denny asked, leaning in closer.

"You and I are going to need to talk about the things going on in your head. Otherwise, this is never going to work."

Raine sighed and tried to decide how much she could tell Denny without revealing the truth. No human would be ok with hearing about their girlfriend, the panther. Raine had never heard a single story of a human being accepting of it. Hell, if the roles were reversed, Raine knew that *she* wouldn't be ok with it. She didn't want to be a shifter, and yet here she was.

"It's nothing," Raine finally said. "At least, it's nothing that you need to be worried about. I'm just thinking about the storm that's due on Friday. It's supposed to be pretty bad and you said that you've planned a camping trip for this weekend – with your brother, right?"

Lies. All lies. That's not why you're worried about her being in the woods on Friday at all, the little voice chided in the back of Raine's mind. It was right. Raine couldn't bear the thought of Denny walking into a group of angry shifters. The energy that night would be entirely animalistic. Any human caught in the way would die. Angry animals would be in control and there would be no human thoughts to be had as pack ties were either broken or made. Raine shook her head again. She didn't want Denny to be in the woods that night.

Denny grinned as she turned and leaned against Raine.

"Yeah," she said. "Josh and I are still going camping. We're bringing a bunch of extra blankets though. You don't need to worry. We always go on the first good snow of the year anyway."

Fear sent Raine's heart racing. She'd been hoping that Denny would call the trip off. Instead, her girlfriend was willing to risk frostbite and a danger that she didn't even know existed.

"What about the animals?" Raine asked deliberately. "Most of them will be looking for shelter as the storm gets worse."

Denny laughed, the sound light and happy as if she didn't have a care in the world about her own safety.

"You need to stop worrying," she answered. "Josh and I will be fine. Besides, if the animals are afraid and looking for shelter, they won't be bothering us at all. You are worrying far too much about what is going to happen and you need to relax. We'll be fine. I promise."

Raine draped her arms over Denny's shoulders and clasped her hands together around her.

"Look," she said, practically begging. "Can you please just promise me that you'll stay home on Friday night? The woods aren't safe in a storm. I can't stand the thought of you not getting back safely on Sunday."

"There's something else going on," Denny insisted. "You haven't cared when I've camped in bad weather before so what's the difference now? Why are you getting so upset about Friday?"

"There's nothing else going on. Just please promise me that you'll stay out of the woods on Friday night. Go on Saturday and stay an extra day instead. You're not working on Monday anyway."

"I have the apartment to myself on Sunday, remember? You're supposed to be coming over so we can have some alone time there."

Raine sighed. She didn't know how else to make Denny see that she shouldn't be in the woods on Friday night. A tight pinching sensation formed in her chest. She needed to come up with a better lie – something that would make Denny think twice. *Everything would be so much easier if I could just tell her the truth*, Raine thought. However, telling

Denny the truth would be to put them both in grave danger.

After a few moments of tense silence, Denny sighed heavily.

"Fine," she said. "I'll tell Josh that we aren't going until Saturday. But when I get home on Monday, I expect you to be naked in my bed."

Raine's cheeks burned as a shy smile spread across her face.

"I think I can manage that," she said.

"You know that I'd do anything for you," said Denny.

She grinned and grabbed Raine's hands, lifting them to her mouth to kiss the back of them.

Raine couldn't shake the horrible feeling that she was still lying to her girlfriend. *Would Denny still do anything for me if she knew what I really was?* she wondered.

Chapter Six

The night the shifters were due to gather in a large clearing deep within the woods, snow was falling in thick sheets. The pack felt confident that no human would be able to stumble upon them, especially not in such awful weather. Raine supposed that one of the good things about being a shifter was in having a resistance to the cold. Shifters were too warm-blooded to be impacted by the snow. Still, Raine put on a black cardigan and some boots; she didn't want the falling snow to soak her and she was keen to be steady on her feet.

She walked out of her room and down the stairs. The door to the meeting room had been left slightly ajar. Quietly, she looked inside to the view of Lucas sitting in a chair. His hands were clasped together in his lap as he looked down at them. Shelly was kneeling in front of him, holding them tightly. Even from where she stood, Raine could see that they were both crying.

She stepped away, wondering what it would feel

like to have somebody love her that much; somebody to sit there with her as she was potentially moments away from death. She wanted that one special person to share the future with her. More than anything, she wished that Denny could be that person. It was impossible though. The likelihood was too high that Denny would be long gone by the time Raine was facing death.

Shaking the thought from her head, Raine walked outside to where the shifters were gathered. Together they would enter the clearing but upon leaving it, at least one of the pack would be dead. The way of the pack had always felt unjust to Raine.

Upon seeing Raine, Dominique sneered.

"When I become leader," she said. "Rainbow's girlfriend will be the first thing to go."

Raine bowed her head as her stomach twisted in knots. She knew that Dominique wasn't just talking about forcing a breakup; the harsh woman would rip Denny limb from limb if given half the chance. Dark fur sprouted along Raine's arms but she couldn't challenge Dominique. Dominique was a better fighter. In fact, if anyone could beat Lucas in a fight, it was Dominique. Other members of the pack believed it too, their eyes becoming tearful as

Lucas walked out with Shelly. The couple's daughter trailed behind them, a dummy in her mouth.

Raine looked at Lucas. Although she didn't get on with him all of the time, he was the closest thing to family that she had ever known. He gave her a subtle nod as Shelly stepped forwards and scooped up their daughter. Children were not spared from seeing a challenge. Shifter children grew up knowing the harsh reality of what it was to be animalistic.

Raine followed along with everyone to the trail that had been worn into the ground by packs long ago. The path led to the sacred fighting grounds; the one place where the leader of the pack could fight their own members on fair footing. There was nothing to be gained from a surprise attack and nobody would respect such a thing. On the sacred fighting grounds, no pack members were allowed to interfere. Those who weren't fighting could only sit on the sidelines and witness the loss of life.

As the group entered the clearing, the storm was getting worse. Snow whirled down around them in bitter pellets of ice. Raine winced as a particularly large piece bounced against her cheek. The wind whipped around the pack, cold but not uncomfortable. Lucas and Dominique stepped into the centre of the clearing as the pack gathered around the edges. Children clung to their parents, their eyes wide. Some of them had never seen a challenge before. Afterwards, they would never be the same again.

There was a snarl from Dominique before she shifted into a ginormous peregrine falcon. She flew high above the pack and circled around the clearing, waiting for her chance as Lucas shifted without a sound into a muscular and stealthy lion. He stood in the snow and watched Dominique fly around. Raine crossed her fingers behind her back and sent up a silent wish for Lucas to win.

Without warning, Dominique twisted, diving towards Lucas. She opened her wings at the last possible moment, digging her claws into his ears. Lucas snarled and snapped at her. He got up on his hind legs and quickly swatted her to the ground with his large front paws. Dominique wasted no time in getting back up and into the air where she was safe.

"This is going to be horrible," Shelly said as she approached Raine.

"Yeah," Raine agreed.

The last thing Raine wanted to do was to stand with

Shelly, the woman who was perhaps about to lose her mate. She had no choice though. The pack was huddled tightly together and now wasn't the time to turn Shelly away.

Lucas ripped Dominique out of the air and tossed her to the ground. Scarlet blood soaked into the blanket of snow that had settled.

"You know that we need to have a chat about your girlfriend," Shelly said, trying to be kind. "If Dominique kills Lucas, you need to get to Denny before she does. You'll both need to make a run for it. If it comes to that, I promise I'll do my best to hold Dominique off for as long as I can."

Raine was speechless for a moment. She had always had Shelly down as being self-absorbed. It shocked her to know that the woman had been paying attention.

"I don't know why you would do that," Raine finally said.

"Do you know why Lucas gives you such a hard time about Denny?"

Lucas roared as Dominique's beak sunk deep into his back. He whirled around but she was already back in the air and flying away as fast as she could.

He got up on his hind legs with his front paws raised. Dominique didn't see him until it was too late. Grabbing her between his paws, he dragged her to the ground. She was wild with rage as she fought her way free once more.

"Because he doesn't agree with me dating a human?" Raine asked.

"You would think that, wouldn't you?" Shelly said, laughing and shaking her head. "It's not that. He gives you a hard time because over time, being with a human would be incredibly difficult for you. You'll outlive her by decades. If Lucas were to take her under the protection of the pack, he would need to be sure that she's worth it. Is she worth it?"

Raine looked away from Shelly. After only a few months of dating, she wasn't ready to tell Denny about who – and what – she was. In fact, she didn't know if she would ever be ready to tell her. With this in mind, Raine didn't feel able to answer Shelly's question.

Raine's thoughts were interrupted when suddenly she caught a glimpse of dark hair and a black leather jacket out of the corner of her eye. Her heart stopped in her chest and time seemed to slow down. There was a human, one who shouldn't be there, standing at the edge of the clearing. Raine wanted to scream and tell her to run but that would certainly put her in danger. Raine's hands shook as she could only hope for the human's attention.

"Denny?!" Raine finally whispered as loudly as she could get away with.

Denny didn't respond, her focus completely on the bloodbath that was taking place before her.

"Yes," said Shelly, laughing again. "That's who we're talking about."

Raine grabbed Shelly's arm, her hands shaking even more as she nodded towards where Denny was stood.

"No," Raine whispered frantically. "Denny is right over there. She's surrounded by shifters who are frothing at the mouth and ready to kill."

"Fuck!" Shelly exclaimed. "You have to get her out of here right now before she gets hurt."

All of a sudden, the focus of the fight changed. Raine felt her whole world turn upside down. She could do nothing but watch as Dominique screeched, her wings flapping hard as she flew directly towards Denny.

Raine screamed and, without giving it a second thought, threw herself forwards. She could hear the sound of her clothes ripping and she could feel the fire flooding through her veins as she completely changed form. The other shifters were changing too, their bloodlust rising. In the heat of the moment, the less experienced ones would be eager to kill.

Raine saw red as she landed steadily on the ground in her panther form. The shift had been painful but she was too scared to acknowledge it. It had been the fastest shift of her life and she only hoped that it would be enough. Through the snow, her claws were firm on the ground. She shoved her way through the shifting people and placed herself in front of Denny.

All that Raine could hear was Denny screaming – shrill and long, as if trapped in a nightmare. She knew that Denny was witnessing a sight of horror like nothing she had ever seen before. There were people turning into animals in front of her; the impossible was happening right before her very eyes. Raine didn't have time to worry about that though. She needed to deal with Dominique, who was determined to kill Denny.

Raine roared and started backing away from the peregrine falcon, forcing Denny to move back with her. Denny was still screaming. *Don't turn and run, Denny*, Raine thought as she kept her eyes focused on the bird. Dominique could fly faster than Raine would be able to run. Not to mention all of the other shifters who were now circling in front of Raine. She was blocking their prey. They would kill her if they had to. When the bloodlust was strong, the pack no longer cared who stood in their way. Whoever it was would be brought down.

Dominique twisted, speeding like a bullet as she fell through the air towards her prey. Raine growled and used her tail to sweep Denny to the side as if she weighed nothing. Although she could hear Denny screaming and scrambling to get up again, Raine couldn't look at her in that moment. She needed to take Dominique out.

Raine growled and jumped into the air. She may not have been the best fighter, but she was able to catch her target with accuracy. As soon as she'd fallen to the ground, she had the huge falcon in a deadly grip. Dominique struggled between Raine's paws but it was no use. Raine held the bird to the ground and ripped out her throat. The shifters could do nothing but stand in silence as Dominique changed from a falcon and back into a woman. Blood stained her naked pale skin and tattered pieces of her throat hung limp. Raine used one big paw to push the dead body to the side.

She snarled as another shifter charged towards her. She had no choice but to meet them halfway, her claws ripping into the wolf's back. She tore out chunks of flesh, her fangs snapping in the other creature's face. She couldn't let Denny get hurt. She had to protect her at all costs.

If she had listened to me in the first place, we wouldn't be in this fucking mess right now!

Raine grabbed the wolf by the throat and held it against the ground. Another wolf came to stand at her side. When Lucas came to stand by her on the other side, Raine released the wolf she was holding and backed away. Lucas and Shelly would take care of the pack. Raine needed to get Denny away from the danger as quickly as she possibly could.

Although Raine walked slowly towards Denny, the human still looked terrified. The sound of Denny's screams tore Raine's heart in two. She hadn't wanted Denny to find out this way.

Carefully using one claw, Raine carved a message into the dirt.

Get on.

Denny looked at the message, tears in her eyes. She shook her head and backed away until she was against a tree. Raine sighed and shook her head before carving another message into the bloodstained snow.

Get on or you will die here. Trust me. It's Raine.

Denny's eyes grew wide and she started shaking her head again. She was hysterical now. It was devastating for Raine to see her like this and there was nothing she could do to make her listen. As Raine quickly looked over her shoulder, she could see that the shifters were locked in battle with each other, claws and teeth slicing through the air and flesh. There was only one option left. It was going to be painful and it was going to drain most of her energy.

Raine closed her eyes and gritted her teeth together. The pain started spreading like wildfire now that she had time to feel it. Her blood was burning hot and her muscles were screaming. Every bone in her body broke and then reformed again. When the shift was finally over, Raine was on the ground, naked and panting from the pain. She looked up at Denny who froze in place, her mouth open as if another scream was about to come out.

"We need to get out of here before you are made into somebody's lunch," Raine addressed Denny in a firm tone. "When I shift back, get on my back and hold on. Do you understand me?"

Before Denny could answer, Raine shifted back into a panther. She stood and shook out her fur. Her chest was still heaving as she stared at Denny, who cautiously walked over and finally jumped on. Raine tried to ignore the pain of how Denny grabbed at the fur between her shoulder blades. It was the only chance they had at getting out alive.

Raine ran through the woods and back to the pack house. She didn't stop running until she was at the shed. When she stopped, Denny hopped off and stared in shock as the panther turned back into her girlfriend, her skin covered in a layer of sweat.

"What are you?" Denny said, her voice wavering as she looked at Raine. "What the hell is all of this? How the fuck do you just keep something like that a secret?"

Raine sighed, the exhaustion setting in.

"I'm naked," she said. "Can I at least get dressed before we start arguing? If you're going to dump me, I'd rather not be naked for it. You really should have listened to me, you know."

"How the fuck are you making jokes right now?"

Raine gave Denny a wry smile as she opened the shed door.

"It comes with pack life," she said.

Upon entering the shed, Raine found that her plastic box was empty. With a sigh, she reached up to the top shelf and grabbed a towel, trying to wipe away all of the blood and sweat from her body. By the time she was done, the white towel had turned the colour of rust. She tossed it into the laundry basket in the corner and looked for Dominique's box. Luckily there was something in there that she could wear. Once she was dressed, Raine walked out of the shed and found Denny curled up against a tree.

Raine crouched down in front of Denny. When she reached out to touch her kindly, Denny jerked away.

"You should go before the rest of the pack gets home," Raine said. "Many of them are going to be worse for wear and healing isn't pretty."

Although it was breaking her heart to do it, Raine turned away from Denny. It was the last thing that she wanted to do but she had always known that it would be coming sooner or later. She could feel the tugging in her chest, the lump rising in her throat, and her eyes burning from unshed tears as she tried to hold them back. She couldn't let the pack see her like this. She didn't even want Denny to see her like this. She needed to be strong enough to end this for the both of them. She looked over her shoulder at Denny, who was getting to her feet.

"You're a monster," Denny said as she stumbled away. "A monster."

Raine entered the house and watched through the window as Denny walked in the direction of the main road. It was only once she was out of sight that Raine allowed the tears to finally fall.

Chapter Seven

A few weeks later, Lucas addressed the pack in the meeting room.

"Whoever is behind the attacks on the humans is becoming bolder in their approach," he said.

Raine stared at the ground. She couldn't be bothered to care about this, or indeed anything else. She felt hollow inside. The only thing that had been worth living for had been ripped away from her. After Denny had left that day, Raine had taken to keeping an eye on her from a distance. She had no idea whether Denny had told anyone about the pack, but she wouldn't care even if she had. Raine knew that she deserved every ounce of anger and hatred that Denny could push her way. She was a monster, a beast that killed. There was nothing more that she could ever be.

"Raine, pay attention," Shelly whispered.

She was sitting next to Raine. She had made it her

personal mission to get Raine back on her feet. Raine didn't understand why Shelly cared about her situation but appreciated the sentiment all the same; some of the pack wouldn't even acknowledge her after she'd killed one of their own to save a human. To them, it was an unthinkably low move.

"There are reports coming in from the police that a wild animal is walking through the town at night," Lucas announced. "Although this could be a wild animal that has come down from the woods – at least that's what the police think – I have followed the trail personally. I'm convinced it's a shifter – one that has gone rogue and has no respect for life."

Shelly nodded along with the words while Raine stared out of the window instead, remembering the night that Denny had showed up. A part of her longed to see the horrible old truck pull up outside again. It would be more than she deserved but there was something that told her to keep wishing. What she and Denny had was special. Her heart didn't understand how it could all be over already. She wanted to get back with Denny, to make things all better. She didn't know if that would ever be possible in view of what had happened though.

"In a week's time, we will go on a hunt for this

shifter. Our pack will bring them here and we will interrogate them," Lucas said, pacing back and forth with his hands clasped behind his back. "We've lost one of our best fighters recently and several more were injured. Therefore, mandatory training will begin for all shifters over the age of eighteen. You will meet me in the back yard every night after sunset and we will train until sunrise. We'll take it in turns to patrol the town through the night."

It scared Raine to think that the shifter could find Denny. Tears burned in her eyes as she mused on the danger that Denny could be in. The scent of shifter would still be on her truck and in her home – all because Raine had been there. The rogue shifter could be drawn to it so easily.

Without saying a word, Raine stood up so forcefully that her chair fell back. It clattered against the floor as she moved across the room to look at the map. The shifter was working in a spiral that started at the edge of town. It was getting closer and closer to the centre, its laps around town becoming smaller with each new missing person. The police could see the pattern but they were missing the motivation behind the attacks. The shifter was looking for one of its own kind. Though it hadn't discovered the pack, it had found Raine's scent all over town.

Raine traced the pattern on the map with a finger as she considered where she had been and where Denny's truck might have travelled. The spiral looked as if it would get tighter. There was maybe a week to go until the shifter would reach the centre.

"Denny's apartment!" Raine whispered.

"What?" Lucas asked. "What is it?"

Raine looked up from the map, her eyes wide. All other eyes in the room were on her. Fire spread across her cheeks as she looked around. Clearing her throat, she looked at Lucas and took a deep breath. Her hands shook as she pointed to the spiral on the map.

"The shifter must be following my scent," she said. "Some of the attacks have happened in the exact same spots that I've frequented with Denny. The spiral is getting tighter and if it maintains this pattern, the shifter will arrive at Denny's apartment. I'm convinced that it's following my scent."

Lucas joined Raine at the map. He studied it and nodded.

"We need to assume that Denny will be one of the

shifter's targets," he asserted. "We need to take her under protection. We also have to assume that the shifter is simply looking for other shifters, and not just Raine in particular."

A voice from the back of the room spoke up. It was Alex.

"Why would the rogue shifter be following Raine's scent?" she asked as she bounced her baby on her knee. "We've all frequented the town within the last few months. The shifter could have picked up on any scent and followed it. Why would it choose Raine's specifically?"

Lucas considered Alex's question for a moment as Raine sat down in an empty chair. She looked down at her hands, lacing her fingers together to try and stop them from shaking. Denny was in danger, and possibly because of her. She sighed and twisted the small opal ring on her finger. All she had wanted to do was to be with Denny. Instead, she may have handed the woman a death sentence.

Shelly stood up and moved to be at Lucas' side.

"Even though we all spend time in the town," she said. "Raine has spent more time there recently – when she was seeing Denny. Due to this, her scent would be the strongest to another shifter."

Raine bent forwards in her chair and buried her face in her hands. All of this was her fault. Denny was in danger. The pack was in danger. If she had never been born, and if she had never been turned into a shifter, this wouldn't be happening. *She* was drawing the rogue shifter in. *She* was the cause of all the deaths and kidnappings that were happening within the town.

"Somebody needs to go and get Denny," said Lucas. "It can't be Raine. If our theory is right, her scent – combined with Denny's – could draw the shifter straight back to the pack house."

Raine peeked through her fingers when she felt hands on her knees. Shelly was crouched in front of her.

"It will be ok," Shelly said in a soothing tone. "We're going to fix this. I'm going to get Denny myself and I will bring her back here, ok?"

"I don't care," Raine whispered, tears trailing down her cheeks. "It doesn't matter anymore. Everybody is in danger and it's because of me."

"We are always in danger. It comes with being a shifter," Shelly said kindly. "I know that you love her and that you never meant to cause any trouble."

"She won't want to see me. She hates me now."

"That's not true," Shelly said. "I've seen how she looks at you. I doubt that she hates you. Hell, if I didn't know any better, I would say that she is deeply in love with you."

Raine shook her head and stood up, stepping away from Shelly.

"I don't care what you do," Raine said, her voice full of emotion. "I plan on avoiding her. It's easier for both of us that way."

Chapter Eight

It was almost midnight when Shelly left the pack house, driving away in her small blue car. Raine sat and watched from her bedroom window. She didn't move until Shelly returned an hour later with Denny, who was slumped in the front seat. From the window, Raine hadn't been able to tell whether Denny was awake or not. With Denny being a fighter and with what she'd seen already, it was plausible that Shelly had needed to be creative in getting her into the car.

Raine walked downstairs and waited by the front door. Moments later, Shelly came through with Denny cradled in her arms. To know that Denny had been tranquilised made Raine feel painfully guilty.

With hindsight now to her advantage, Raine cursed herself for how she'd failed to anticipate that it would come to this. Still, she walked out to Shelly's car and gathered Denny's bags. Shelly carried Denny upstairs and into the room next to

Raine's. Raine frowned but said nothing, setting the bags inside the room before leaving.

Escaping Shelly and her infinite list of questions had never been easy. Moments after Raine had flopped onto her bed, Shelly entered the room with her hands on her hips. Cocking an eyebrow, she waited. Raine refused to talk though. As far as she was concerned, there was no more talking about Denny to be done.

Finally, Shelly sighed and then sat on the edge of Raine's bed. With a groan, Raine rolled over onto her stomach and tried to pretend that the conversation that was about to happen was only in her imagination.

"You were only young when Lucas and I took you in," Shelly said. "I'll never forget that stray child who showed up on our doorstep, covered in blood and crying for her parents. To this day we still have no idea how you knew where to go. Maybe it was destiny. You were still human back then, I'm sure you remember."

"Yeah," Raine said. "I don't know how I got there either. That night was the most painful I've ever had."

"Well, you were only ten at the time. The best I

could get out of you was that your parents were both drug addicts and that you had been living on the street. Sometimes I wonder what life would have been like for you if Lucas hadn't changed you."

Raine scoffed and rolled over to look at Shelly.

"I've spent the last thirteen years wondering the exact same thing," she said sadly. "Would I have ended up like my mother? Maybe that would have been better for me. As a shifter, I can't fall in love with who I want to. I hate it."

"Lucas still hasn't forgiven himself for that," Shelly answered honestly. "Neither have you, I see. You *will* find somebody to love. You could change them into a shapeshifter – if that's what you both wanted."

"Why would I wish this lifestyle on anyone else?" Raine said, her tone laced with frustration. "Why the fuck would I want to turn somebody else into a monster? Where they would have to kill or be killed to survive?"

"It's not as simple as that, Raine. You want somebody to spend the rest of your life with you. You might not find that among our people. I say *our people* because you're one of us. Whether you like it or not, Lucas did what he thought was needed to make sure that you would survive."

Raine's eyes watered as she shook her head and rolled back over onto her stomach. She buried her face in her pillow as she sobbed. She had never wanted this life. There would be hell to pay if she even thought about turning Denny. As much as Raine wanted to be with her, this was not a life that she would choose to give to anyone, least of all someone she loved.

"I know from my own experiences that you have to make the most of what you have, regardless of the circumstances," Shelly said.

The dip in the bed shifted as she stood up. Raine heard her open the bedroom door and walk out into the hallway.

Once Shelly had closed the door behind her, Raine was alone with her thoughts again. She rolled onto her back and stared up at the ceiling. If the pack was going to keep Denny under their protection, it would be impossible to avoid seeing her. Raine reasoned that at best, she would need to be civil towards Denny. Besides, Denny would need a familiar face in her life whilst living with monsters for an undetermined amount of time.

With a sigh, Raine got up and went out into the hallway. She stood at the door of what was now Denny's room. She could hear the sound of breathing but it wasn't deep enough for Denny to be asleep; she was probably awake and terrified. Upon hearing the sound of Denny's sobs, her heart broke all over again.

Bracing herself, Raine started to undo the lock that was keeping Denny trapped inside the room.

"I don't think that now is the time to go in there."

Raine let go of the lock. Her heart racing, she spun around to look at Lucas. He was right. This wasn't the time to see Denny.

"You look exhausted," he said kindly. "At least get cleaned up a little bit first. She needs a familiar face soon. She was kidnapped from her home in the middle of the night and she has no clue what's going on."

Raine nodded and disappeared back into her room. After a quick shower, she pulled on a pair of leggings and a loose tank top. She left her hair wet and curly. It clung to her back in thick waves. Taking a moment to steady her breathing, she made her decision: she needed to talk to Denny and put things right before they could get any worse.

Once she was out in the hall, Raine winced as she opened the door to Denny's room. Denny's wide eyes found her straight away. Raine felt like she was on fire as Denny's gaze slowly trailed up and down her body.

"What have you done to me now?" Denny asked, her voice wavering and quaking with each word. "What do you want from me?"

Raine sighed and sat down in the armchair.

"Where do you want me to start?" she asked.

"For once," said Denny. "I want you to just tell me the truth."

Raine nodded and clasped her hands together, looking down at them.

"I guess we should start from the very beginning then," she said. "I haven't always been this way; I wasn't born a shapeshifter. I used to be a normal human."

"I don't believe you," Denny said doubtfully.

"I know it's a lot to take in, really I do," said Raine. "I've been lying to you for months about who I am and more importantly, *what* I am. I didn't start off this way though. As a little girl, I was living on the streets with my parents. One night, they were attacked.”

Raine paused and looked around the room. It had been years since she'd talked to anybody about what had happened. Not even Lucas and Shelly knew the full story. Sure, she had told them most of it, but some parts had just been too upsetting to recall.

“It was only after the attack that I realised I was covered in my parents' blood. It had all happened so quickly. I'm still not sure who or *what* got to them but I had never seen anything like it before. As soon as I heard the sounds of scratching and biting, I ran away. My parents were pretty out of it already. I couldn't save them. I'm a coward, Denny.”

Denny got up off the bed and slowly walked towards Raine, who was crying. She gave her a much-needed cuddle and even planted a gentle kiss on her forehead.

“It's not your fault, Raine,” she whispered. “You were only a kid. What could you have done?”

“I don't know… I…”

"Shh..." Denny soothed. "You don't have to tell me everything right now."

"We need to talk about this," Raine said. "You always said that we should talk more."

Denny made a noncommittal noise in the back of her throat, planting a few more kisses onto Raine's forehead. As the two women held each other tightly, Raine groaned, wriggling beneath Denny. It had been too long since they had last touched and they were both aching for release.

"Bed," Denny said, confidently taking control. "Now."

"We'll talk later," Raine said. "Right now though, I'm glad you're here."

Chapter Nine

At sunrise the following morning, Denny held Raine's naked body in an affectionate embrace. As daylight broke through the curtains, Raine pulled away and sat up in bed, wrapping the duvet around her chest. She looked at Denny, admiring the beauty of the little freckles around her nose. It made her feel emotional as she got out of bed and went to sit back in the armchair.

"Where do you think you're going?" Denny asked, her voice raspy with sleep. "Get back here."

It was almost enough to tempt Raine back into bed.

"No," said Raine. "The sex was amazing but we need to talk about what brought you here, and what the next steps will be moving forward."

"Fine," Denny said as she got out of bed and started to get dressed. "You want to talk; then let's start with the other people here – who are definitely not your family. I'm here because they kidnapped me. Is that what you really want to talk about right now?"

Raine looked away from Denny and began searching the floor for her own clothing. Once she was dressed, she sat back down in the armchair. Twisting the ring on her finger back and forth, she looked up at Denny with tears in her eyes.

I don't want to cry in front of her, Raine thought as she gathered the remaining courage that she had left.

"You were brought here because somewhere out there, there is a shifter who is tracking our scent."

"Our scent?!" Denny exclaimed. "You have got to be fucking kidding me. I was kidnapped because of you?!"

She shook her head in frustration, scrunching her hands into fists in her hair as she sat on the bed.

"I guess you could say that," Raine explained. "The sooner you talk about this with me like a rational adult though, the sooner we can work through it."

"What is there to work through? I'm in this crazy situation because of you and I'm just supposed to be ok with it?!"

"If you had just stayed out of the damn woods that night, everything would have been ok. You wouldn't have seen this side of me and you wouldn't have been in danger. But no, you didn't listen to me because you thought you knew better."

"So what? You didn't plan on telling me that every now and then, you turn into a giant cat?!"

Raine got up and stormed across the room. She was growing tired of playing this game and Denny was beyond reasonable when she was worked up like this. Though Raine hadn't known her for long, she knew that they were never going to get anywhere if Denny kept being so hot-headed.

With a firm hand, Raine turned Denny's face towards hers.

"You're going to listen to me, Denny. What I'm about to say is probably going to save your life, which means that I need you to listen to me no matter how much you want to tell me to fuck off. I messed up. I did it because I really care about you. It felt kinder to lie to you knowing that you and I would never be able to have a life together."

"You want a life with me?"

Raine sighed and pinched the bridge of her nose as her cheeks flushed a dark pink. This wasn't how she'd wanted to reveal things to Denny. Being a shapeshifter was ruining her life yet again. She needed to discuss the potential death that was looming over both of their heads but Denny was now fixating on Raine's feelings for her. It was so much to be dealing with – for both of them. Raine didn't know if it was even possible to share her life with a human in the long run. She had never heard of a shifter who had managed to do it successfully; they either had to change their partner into a shifter or face being alone again when they outlived the human.

"Why do you care about that part of it right now?" Raine finally said as she sat down on the edge of the bed. "If you think I'm a monster, then surely what I feel for you doesn't matter?"

"You think you're a monster too," Denny said as she shuffled away from Raine and deeper into the pillows on the bed. "And anyway, I'm allowed to care about what you think of me. I mean, this is all too much to handle and I'm hoping that I'll wake up to find that it's all just one big nightmare. But what if I don't wake up? What if this is really happening? Where does that leave us?"

"I had assumed that there would no longer be an

us," Raine said. "There's a lot you don't understand about what it is to be a shifter. Fuck, Denny, I've killed in cold blood before. What if I got upset and hurt you too?"

Raine felt the gentle weight of Denny's hand settle on her shoulder.

"What if *I* got upset and hurt *you*?" Denny said softly. "I know this is a lot to take in and we haven't even been together for half a year yet. Hell, we haven't been talking for the last few weeks. You and I are something different though. I feel it so strongly and have been hoping that you do too."

Raine sighed and shrugged Denny's hand away. She twisted around to look at her. Denny was strong; the kind of woman who wouldn't let anybody take advantage of her. She was hard and took no shit but she was kind. Sweet. Too innocent for this world in some ways.

"Ok," said Raine. "Let's imagine for a moment that you could look past the fact that I'm a shifter, or indeed, even accept that about me. What happens then?"

Denny bit her bottom lip and ran a hand through her hair. She couldn't look at Raine. She was struggling to gather her thoughts and there were tears in her eyes. Raine meanwhile, knew that she would never recover from the heartbreak of having to end it with Denny. She felt strongly that Denny deserved to be happy though; to live a good life and to grow old with another human. To love somebody who wasn't also a wild animal.

"I want to know everything. Every detail," Denny spoke suddenly. "You and I are something. I'm not sure what yet, but I think that it could be something really good. I love *who* you are."

She loves me. It's impossible, but she says that she does, Raine thought, her heart fluttering as time came to a standstill. She wanted to shove the small glimmer of hope away though. She didn't want to be so selfish as to string Denny along. She wanted Denny to be truly happy.

Raine looked at Denny and was once again taken aback by her beauty. It was impossible not to be in love with her. She was so strong, intelligent and open-minded. Raine knew that the only way this could work would be for her to respect Denny enough to give her the whole truth, and to let her make her own mind up from there. She needed to put the ball in Denny's court; no more lies, no more half-truths.

"I know we need to talk about this," Denny

continued. "If we decide to go forward with a relationship – which I admit I'm hesitant about – I need to know everything. Every little bit of what our future would look like together. Are you with me on this?"

Raine nodded. There were many points that she could start with. There were so many things that she could say about what their life would look like together. After a few moments of weighing up where to start, she decided that the end would be the best.

"I will outlive you. Significantly. I'm talking at least fifty years but probably closer to a hundred. We'd reach a point in our lives where people would mistake you for being my mother, and then eventually my grandmother. The dynamic of our relationship would inevitably change."

Denny played with a loose thread on her shirt as she mulled everything over. Raine had moved from sitting on the bed to sitting on the floor with her back against the armchair. It was easier to talk about the future with some physical distance between them. Raine smiled wryly to herself as she thought about how it would have perhaps been easier to write everything down in a letter. At least that way, she wouldn't have to see the expressions on Denny's face as she worked hard to comprehend the scale of the situation.

"So you'd have to be my carer when I'm too old to look after myself? I couldn't ask that of you, Raine."

"Of course I'd take care of you, Den. I'll always want to take care of you – even if you need to call time on us being a couple."

"That makes you sound like a stalker," Denny said, her laughter softening the heavy mood of the conversation.

Raine smiled but she was still upset. She had meant every word; she would always want to look out for Denny. The pack knew that Denny was aware of them and they would be watching her to make sure she kept her mouth shut. If needed, the pack would intervene. A chill ran up Raine's spine when she thought about what a pack intervention would look like. It wouldn't be good for anyone involved.

Denny's brows knitted together as she crawled to the end of the bed and turned to rest on her stomach.

"What's wrong?" she asked. "You look like you've just seen a ghost."

"The pack would kill you if you were to tell anybody about them."

The colour drained from Denny's face. Her hands shook against the quilt on the bed as she grabbed a pillow and clutched it tightly. Finally, she nodded slowly and took a deep breath.

"I understand," she said. "It's barbaric but I understand, I think."

"If you were to tell anybody about the shifters, you wouldn't be believed anyway. To be on the safe side though, the pack would have no option but to kill you," Raine elaborated. "We have to protect our own above all else."

"You would kill me," Denny confirmed.

It wasn't a question. It didn't even matter if it was. Raine didn't have the right answer but if it came down to it, she knew what the pack would expect her to do. She knew that she wouldn't be given a choice. It was a painful truth, but a truth nonetheless.

Chapter Ten

There was a scream from downstairs followed by the sound of breaking glass. Raine jumped up and looked at Denny. She could hear the frantic pounding of feet in the hallway.

As dark fur started to sprout from Raine's arms, she spoke firmly to Denny.

"I need you to stay in this room. Push something heavy against the door and keep away from the window. Unless it's me or Lucas, you mustn't let *anyone* in the room. Understood?"

Denny said nothing, her eyes wide as another scream echoed in the hallway. Raine charged forwards and grabbed Denny's chin passionately, forcing her to pay attention. Denny blinked slowly, as if in a daze.

"Denny, I need you to do as I say right now."

"Ok. Yeah," Denny said, clearly still bewildered.

Raine let go of Denny's chin, her hands beginning to sprout into claws. She wasn't fast enough when pulling away though. Tears stung her eyes as she noticed the thin line of blood forming on Denny's chin.

"I'm so sorry," she whispered.

She darted out of the bedroom, slamming the door behind her. When she got downstairs, there was broken glass and blood on every surface imaginable. Not only that, but there were several dead bodies too. She didn't have time to think as she threw herself between a snarling coyote and Shelly's daughter. Sharp teeth closed around Raine's arm as her clothes were shredded from her body. As she shifted, she was able to tear her arm free. She kept herself between the child and the coyote. White foam poured out of the beast's mouth and thick globules of drool fell to the ground. Raine growled and snapped her teeth together when the coyote tried to advance.

This must have something to do with the kidnappings, Raine thought as she used her tail to keep Lissa away from the coyote. With her eyes focused on the enemy, Raine briefly wondered where the hell Lucas and Shelly could be. To the edge of her field of vision, she could see several other coyotes pouring in through the smashed windows. Her heart started to pound more urgently as the first coyote lunged forwards. She caught the monster by its front paw between her jaws, eventually flipping it onto its back.

Something solid landed at Raine's side. She tumbled from the force, a gap opening between herself and Lissa. Snarling, she got to her feet, her tail swishing from side to side as she looked between the pair of coyotes coming towards her.

"I've got her," a soft voice said.

Raine looked over her shoulder to see that Denny had scooped Lissa up and was now holding her tightly. Raine froze in fear, just long enough for a set of sharp teeth to latch onto her ear.

With a scream, she blindly swung a paw and felt the weight of the impact beneath it. As the coyote whimpered in pain, she was on top of it within seconds. She needed to protect Lissa and Denny. She snarled before ripping out the throat of the coyote. The moment its body went limp, she turned to look for another one.

A coyote was following Denny up the stairs, rapidly gaining on her. Raine tried to catch up to it but she was too slow. She watched in horror as the coyote wrapped its jaws around Denny's ankle.

The pain made Denny drop Lissa on the landing.

Denny screamed as a trio of coyotes jumped in front of Raine. As Raine tried to fight them off, Denny had no choice but to limp out of the pack house and off into the darkness. With Denny outside, Raine lost control. She snarled, her jaws snapping together as she bit and scratched at anything within her reach. She didn't stop. She only saw red as she tried to kill everything in sight. She needed to make the house safe for Denny.

The only thing that succeeded to pierce through Raine's bloodlust was the sound of Lissa's cry. Raine turned and urgently ran up the stairs. Quickly, she looked the child over. There was a small cut on her cheek but she was otherwise unharmed. Denny had saved Lissa's life. It was up to Raine to keep them both safe now.

Raine stood in front of the child but no more coyotes came. It was the first time that she'd had a moment to notice just how much blood had soaked into her fur. With a heaving chest, she shifted back into her human form and tried to ignore the pain. She needed to go and find Denny, who was probably still outside.

Lucas' voice boomed through the house.

"Pack meeting in ten minutes," he commanded. "And where the fuck are Lissa and Shelly?"

"I've got Lissa here!" Raine called out as she scooped up the child.

In a matter of seconds, Lucas was dashing up the stairs to snatch his daughter away and hold her close. Raine could see the tears running down his face, creating clean tracks through the blood and dirt. Lissa sobbed into her father's shoulder.

"Thank you," Lucas said as he finally looked up at Raine.

"Don't thank me," Raine said. "Denny saved her."

Lucas nodded, his face growing solemn.

"Get dressed," he said. "We need to discuss our next steps."

Raine scowled. She didn't want to talk about next steps. She still needed to know where Denny was and if she was ok.

As soon as Raine got to her room, she slammed the door shut behind her and started pacing. The coyotes could be anywhere by now but it was doubtful that they would have left the town.

Although they were fast, the town wasn't small.

As she got dressed, she looked at the picture of Denny that she had taped to the mirror. Denny had posed for her when they'd had a day out to the apple orchard. It was cheesy and dumb but Raine loved looking at it.

The more Raine stared at the picture, the worse she felt, as if the world as she knew it was about to end.

Once she was ready to face the pack, she walked down the stairs. There would be no going after the coyotes alone. There could be many more of them. She would need the strength of the pack behind her. Denny had saved Lissa, and Raine was certain that Lucas would be willing to rescue her, eradicating the coyotes in the process.

Chapter Eleven

The meeting room was noisier than usual. There was a pile of first aid supplies on the middle of the table. Shifters were helping each other with bandages whilst consoling those who had lost somebody. Fortunately, not everyone had been at the house during the attack. It was the only thing that had prevented more casualties.

Lucas paced the room as he spoke.

"We need to find out where the coyotes came from, and what they want from us," he said. "It's now clear that they were not simply tracking the scent of another shifter. It's more than that. Whilst we can't be certain what they might do next, I will be damned if I'm going to let anything happen to my pack again."

Raine looked at the map of the town as she took her seat. Slowly, she scanned over every location, counting the ones where people had been taken from. A chill swept through her entire body.

"We have to find these rogue shifters and we'll make them pay for what they've done," Lucas continued. "Not only have they killed members of our pack in cold blood, but they have also stolen one of our own. It's unforgivable. We will go after these creatures and we will rip them limb from limb."

The sound of supportive cheers echoed around the table. Others had questions. Whispers spread from one person to the next. Raine smiled despite the situation. Lucas had referred to Denny as one of the pack. The other shifters would have no choice but to accept her now.

"We can assume that there are at least twenty in the enemy pack. We outnumber them by nearly double. What we don't know, and what we have not trained for though, is how skilled they could be. Our practice sessions have fallen short; many of you have failed to attend them."

Lucas shot a pointed glance at Raine. Awkwardly, she looked down at her hands.

"That doesn't matter now," Lucas said, keen to move on. "As soon as this meeting is called to a close, we will begin looking for the coyotes. Does anybody else have anything to add?"

Lucas looked around the room but none of the shifters had anything to say. Most were saying goodbye to their loved ones, preparing to leave their children behind with two of the pack's best fighters. If anything were to happen to the pack, there would be a legacy to carry on.

"Very well," Lucas said. "You are all dismissed. Raine, I would like to have a word with you for a minute."

Raine frowned. She was keen to get outside and start looking for Denny. She was desperate to save her. She couldn't bear the thought of her being killed – or turned into a shifter against her will.

"Fuck!" Raine whispered as she looked up at Lucas. "I know where the coyotes are coming from!"

Lucas looked at her for a moment before turning his attention back to the map. His eyes widened and his hands clenched into fists at his side. As soon as Raine had said it, he'd realised what she meant. The coyotes were the eleven missing people; they had been turned into shifters by whoever was the mastermind behind all of this. The rogue shifter must have been working to build a pack of their own over the last few weeks. Raine cursed herself for not having realised it when she had seen the sheer number of coyotes during the attack.

"Shit!" she said. "I should have known."

"You know," Lucas said reassuringly. "You may not be the best fighter, but your mind is a valuable asset to this pack. Remind me to put you on the war council when this is all over."

"Sure," Raine replied. "*If* we get through this."

"You and I will search the location of where we believe the first attack happened," Lucas instructed. "Shortly after that child went missing, the parents moved into a new house. They couldn't bear the memories. I bet there's a shifter there now."

"Why do you think they came here?" she asked.

"I don't know," Lucas answered. "But I would bet my life on it having something to do with you."

Raine's eyes burned. It all felt like it was her fault. She watched as Lucas paced the room again. He gave a nod and she followed him out of the house and into his truck. As he drove, she hoped they could get to Denny and save her before the worst happened. Raine would happily spend the rest of her life trying to make it up to her.

Finally they parked on the road, a good few metres away from the abandoned house. It stood to reason that the first attack had happened there. It was large with no neighbouring houses to either side of it, and it backed out onto the edge of the woods.

"Lucas," Raine said. "What makes you so sure that this has something to do with me?"

He shrugged, the dim light from the moon streaming in through the truck window and illuminating the side of his face.

"Lately, it has seemed as if all of the trouble is connected to you," he explained. "Not to be rude or anything like that, but since Denny came into your life, things have been going wrong. *I* think it's great that you've found her, but *someone* out there doesn't."

Raine got out of the truck and tucked her hands into the pockets of her jeans.

"Who could that be?" she asked. "I killed Dominique."

"She's not the only shifter to have ever had an opinion," Lucas said.

As he got out of the truck and shut the door behind

him, he made sure to leave the windows down. It could come in handy if there wasn't enough time to open a door later.

Raine nodded. There was no way of knowing who was after her or what they wanted. Until she could confront them, it was all guesswork and mystery. More than one person could be holding a grudge against her. They could want something from her. Hell, for all she knew it could have something to do with the death of her parents. She had only found out years after their deaths that they owed a lot of money to a prolifically violent gang. Although it was a long time ago now, she couldn't afford to rule anything out.

Whilst Lucas walked towards one side of the house, Raine headed in the direction of the other. An older building, it had been in disrepair long before the parents of the victim had abandoned it. There was still yellow police tape everywhere. Blood stained the grass and the outside walls of the house. Windows were broken and a haunting wail drifted through the trees. Raine listened to the wind rattle the boards of the porch. They creaked beneath her feet despite how quiet she was trying to be.

On this occasion, she felt thankful for her enhanced senses. After a few moments of listening carefully, she could hear movement coming from somewhere inside the house. The sound wasn't close. Whoever it was, had to be underground somewhere.

Raine looked over at Lucas and waved. Upon managing to get his attention, she pointed towards the truck. Stealthily, they both crept back to it to hold a brief meeting.

"What is it?" Lucas asked, continuing to keep an eye on the house. "Did you hear something?"

"There's somebody in there – possibly more than one person. I think I heard several sets of breathing and at least two different hearts beating. We could be walking into a trap. Maybe we should wait for backup."

Be brave, Denny's voice whispered in Raine's mind. *Now's not the time to back down. Own your trauma. Find me.*

Raine shook her head and stared at the house for a moment.

"Raine, are you ok?" Lucas asked as he touched her shoulder. "You know as well as I do that we'll never get another chance to surprise them like this. They think that we're still back at the pack house licking our wounds."

"I know," Raine said.

She started walking towards the house and then looked back over her shoulder at Lucas.

"Are you coming, or do I need to kick arse by myself?" she whispered theatrically.

Lucas laughed and jogged to be at her side.

"Being around Denny is doing you some good," he said.

Moments later, the duo fell silent. Lucas pulled out his phone and sent a quick message to Shelly but there was no time to do anything else. It was now or never. Raine sensed that Denny was waiting for her.

Own your trauma, she thought to herself. *You are a monster. You will make them fear you.*

Chapter Twelve

The inside of the house was in a troubled state. It was clear to see that the family who had lived there hadn't been in a good way – even before they'd been attacked. In fact, it reminded Raine of her childhood. The peeling wallpaper was stained with cigarette smoke. The laminate kitchen worktop had melted in places where joints had been extinguished. She could see needles and spoons next to lighters that were probably empty.

Cupboard doors hung loose on their hinges and blood soaked the carpets. Whoever had suffered here must have fought like hell. Raine hoped that if there was somebody in the house waiting to perform an ambush, she would be able to take them on. The aura of the house was so threatening that it was difficult to distinguish between fear and the reality of what could happen next.

Lucas motioned to Raine before pointing at a door – the one to the basement. She nodded and gestured for him to go first. With a scowl, he opened the door slowly and quietly. He then carefully started to head down the stairs. Raine took a deep breath and followed him into the darkness.

As they continued to descend, Raine was beginning to suspect that they were heading into an exceptionally deep basement. In a normal home, they would have already reached the lowest point. There were definitely voices coming from down below. As they grew louder, Raine realised how much she and Lucas had overestimated their potential to take on the enemy – they were wildly outnumbered.

Each step into the darkness felt like a death sentence. There was no light to guide them, just the voices. Raine reached out and put her hand on Lucas' shoulder. She didn't want to lose him.

Finally, they reached the end of the stairs and could see dim rays of light against the floor. In front of them were several alcoves. Coming from one to the right there was nothing but noise – it had to be the sound of the enemy coyote shifters, snarling and laughing. It was far too distinctive to be anything else. To the left, there was no sound. *Could Denny be here somewhere?* Raine wondered, afraid but hopeful.

She motioned to Lucas to follow behind her. They

both felt strongly that her senses were on high alert and that it would be foolish to ignore them.

After having checked several rooms, all of which were empty, Raine's heart sank in her chest when she realised that there were only a few more to explore. She believed deeply that Denny had to be somewhere in the basement. There was no way that whoever had kidnapped her would want her to escape. If she'd been turned into a shifter, her captors wouldn't want to give her the chance to turn on them either.

There was still hope that if Denny had been kidnapped, she hadn't been turned into a shifter. Raine reminded herself that it was a foolish hope though. If the coyote leader was set on making as many disciples as possible, Denny wouldn't be spared.

At least if Denny has been turned, she'll have a better chance of being able to defend herself.

Taking a deep breath and trying not to dwell on her fears, Raine entered another room. Through the darkness, there was a subtle light coming in through a window that was far above their heads. Underneath it, there was Denny, curled up on a small dirty mattress. There was a thick chain wrapped around both of her ankles. Raine's eyes followed along the length of it to find that it was buried deep into the wall.

"Lucas," she whispered. "Whoever is behind this has been planning it for a long time. Usually, it would take years not only to figure something like this out, but to execute it so damn well. Even the way that the basement has been expanded would normally have taken years to do – and to get it all done without being noticed must have taken one hell of a lot of work. It makes sense now; the rogue shifter must have needed to turn a lot of people in order to make this all possible in such a short amount of time."

They both moved quietly to get closer to Denny. Lucas spoke in an even quieter whisper.

"If we're quick," he said. "We could get Denny out of here without being noticed."

Raine brushed the hair away from Denny's face, whose chest was rising and falling in shallow breaths.

"I love you," Raine whispered to her.

Denny's hair was tangled in knots. Scratches covered her arms. Rage charged through every fibre of Raine's being as she started to truly acknowledge what Denny had been reduced to. She would find the coyote responsible for this and she would make them pay for what they had done.

Just as Raine was about to storm out of the room to tear out some throats, Lucas put a hand on her shoulder. With a resigned sigh, she nodded and bent down to take a closer look at Denny's ankles. There was pus and blood dripping from the one that the shifter had taken a bite from. Raine sniffed the air but there was no scent of shifter venom in the blood.

Thank fuck, she thought to herself as she got to work on the chain.

The absence of shifter venom meant that Denny hadn't been turned into a shifter. She was still fully human. Of course, that meant that she would still be more vulnerable in a fight than Raine or Lucas. The thought scared Raine. Should the situation come to another fight, Denny wouldn't be able to help and would need protection at every turn.

Raine growled softly, dark hair sprouting on her arms. Sweat beaded on her forehead as she concentrated on a single finger. She watched as the nail elongated and grew into a claw with a deadly curve. After looking over her shoulder, she inserted the claw into the lock near Denny's ankles, twisting it around for a moment before finally hearing a satisfying click. The lock popped open and the chain fell away.

"What are you doing here?" Denny asked.

Raine looked up and smiled.

"Rescuing you."

Denny scowled, clearly not happy about the fact that she needed to be rescued. In fact, she seemed a little delirious, probably from the shock of everything that had already happened to her.

"Fuck off," she said. "My head is pounding. Can we go home?"

Raine placed the back of her hand on Denny's forehead.

"How are you feeling?" she asked. "You don't have a fever at the moment but there's a high risk of infection. That bite looks nasty."

"It didn't feel too good either," Denny said, almost amused. "I was pretty sure my ankle was going to be ripped right from my body."

"Now's not the time for a catch-up," Lucas

commanded. "We need to get out of here."

A throat cleared and a voice spoke from behind them.

"I'm afraid it's too late for that."

Chapter Thirteen

In absolute shock, Raine stared at the familiar woman in the doorway. *Mother?! I thought you were dead!*

"What the fuck?!" Raine exclaimed. "How the fuck are you still alive?"

The woman laughed mockingly and started walking towards Raine, who moved to stand in front of Denny. Lucas positioned himself as a barrier between the woman and Raine. It was clear that Raine had much resentment towards her mother and if challenged, would certainly attack – especially in order to defend Denny.

The woman grinned, revealing teeth that had been sharpened into points.

"Is that any way to talk to your mother?" she chided. "I would have thought that in nearly a decade and a half, you would have picked up some better manners but clearly, you haven't."

Raine growled, her hands shaking and turning into paws. The pain was like nothing she had ever felt before. She didn't care. She needed the pain. In her mind, she *deserved* the pain. It was her fault that everyone was hurt or grieving for their loved ones. It was her fault that so many innocent people had been taken from their families and doomed to a life of killing. If Raine needed to kill her mother in order to prevent anyone else from having to suffer, she would willingly do it.

"You're not my mother. You're just a junkie who had a baby," Raine said, snarling. "Let us go and I will let you live."

By now, the woman's pack had started to make their presence known. They stood behind her, ready to protect their leader.

"Darling, whilst that's very sweet of you, there's no need to worry about me," the woman said in a sarcastic tone. "*You* are the one who is in danger. *You* are the one who will die."

Raine and Lucas moved further back as the woman walked closer towards them. Raine made sure to keep Denny shielded. She was determined to fight to the very end if it would give Denny a chance to run.

"Why are you doing this?" Lucas asked the woman, his voice soft and low.

If he thought that playing the nice guy would work on Raine's mother, he was sorely mistaken. Raine had never known another person so full of hatred. Her mother was one of a kind. Raine had always been a little scared of her. Maybe running away that night all those years ago hadn't been such a bad move after all. She'd been feeling so guilty for years but really, she was beginning to believe for the first time that truly, she didn't owe her mother anything.

"Your father didn't make it when we were attacked by a shifter all those years ago," said the woman. "I did though. They turned me and I've been better for it ever since. I came back stronger. I came back *fighting*. I managed to live under the radar for years but when I heard on the grapevine that you'd fallen for a human, I knew that I had to get rid of you. You were always pretty dumb as a kid and clearly, you haven't evolved much as a shifter either."

Raine screamed and saw red. Darting past Lucas, she charged towards her mother. Screams echoed through the room. As she slashed her claws at her target, Raine couldn't tell whether the screams were coming from her mother or from Denny. It didn't matter to her in that moment. As blood spurted in all directions, she was soon surrounded by coyotes.

In full panther form by that point, teeth and claws tore into Raine but she gave as good as she got. She was so primitively angry that she wasn't deterred by how the enemy outnumbered her greatly. She snarled and screamed as she pounced on one and ripped out its throat. She grabbed another and tore off its muzzle. Blood covered her fur and sinew hung between her teeth.

For every coyote that she killed, another four appeared to take its place. Raine moved backwards, trying to keep the oncoming army from getting to Denny. She screamed as three coyotes got far too close. Seconds later, a lion threw one of the approaching coyotes against a wall. Raine's chest heaved as she looked at her mother. Though the woman was torn open and bleeding, she hadn't bothered to shift; this was a game to her – just like everything else had been.

Raine knew that the fight would be in her favour. She almost pitied her mother for how she was willing to put game-playing above her own life. *So be it*, Raine told herself. *That's her choice.* She charged at her mother again but the woman was fast, moving to the side and grabbing Raine by the tail to brutally plunge a knife into it.

Pain radiated through Raine's body as she pulled back her lips to reveal her fangs. With her ears pressed flat against her head, she circled around her mother. The blood loss was making little black spots dance around her vision. She couldn't give up though. Not now. They were so close to being free.

At least, that's what her mind kept telling her as she was attacked from all sides whilst Lucas defended Denny. Denny's screams and sobs echoed throughout the room as Raine lunged for her mother again.

Before Raine could reach her mother, the woman turned and ran. Even in human form, she was fast. Raine was at her heels though. She chased the woman up the stairs out of the basement, through the house, and into the back yard.

Raine breathed a small sigh of relief when suddenly she could see members of her own pack coming towards the house from the woods. Led by Shelly, they charged into the house, snapping and snarling, and ready to help.

"You know, Rainbow," her mother said. "I thought I'd raised you better than this. But here you are; the kind of person who would kill their own mother. I expected better of you, I really did."

To hear her mother call her by her full name was the final straw for Raine. She screamed, the sound echoing out into the surrounding woods. She pounced at her mother, her paws going for the throat. With a cry of agony, the woman was taken to the ground, thrashing around in a frantic attempt to escape. Raine had rage on her side though. With her full weight on the target and with livid aggression fuelling her, she tore her mother's torso to ribbons and then snapped her neck, eventually tossing the head off to the side.

She'll never be able to harm anybody again, Raine told herself.

As she stumbled away from the remains of her mother, everything within her field of vision started to go dark. The last thing she heard before hitting the ground was Denny screaming.

Chapter Fourteen

When Raine opened her eyes, she was in her room at the pack house. She slowly sat up and looked around. There was no indication of what day it was, or what had happened after she had lost consciousness. She groaned, pain running from one end of her body to the other and back again.

The bedroom door hit the wall as Denny came rushing in.

"What the fuck are you doing, Raine?" she demanded. "Get back in bed and rest. You almost fucking died and I'm not having you tear out a stitch because your stupid arse wants to look around."

"I love you," Raine said, laughing and falling back against her pillows.

The room fell silent. It was unusual for Denny to take a pause in being so outspoken.

"What did you just say?" she asked.

"I love you," Raine said again.

"Well, you damn well better after all the stress that you put me through back there. Do you know how many times I pissed myself watching that damn fight? And then poor Lucas had to carry me out of there – completely soaked in piss – because I couldn't fucking walk."

Raine laughed until tears were streaming down her cheeks. It had been truly horrible but it was the way that Denny described it that cracked her up.

"Oh no," Raine said, joking a little. "That part of it must have been really horrible for you."

Denny limped over to the bed and climbed in beside Raine.

"Yeah, it was. Don't you *ever* do anything like that again or I swear I'll…"

"You'll what?" Raine said cheekily, grinning and then planting a kiss on Denny's forehead.

"No. Shut up and let me finish my threat," said Denny. "If you ever pull any sort of stupid stunt like that again, I will break up with you. For real.

No being a heroic panther and saving my arse from your crazy mother will save the relationship next time. You'd better believe it!"

Even though it caused new waves of pain to blossom in her ribs, Raine couldn't help but chuckle.

"Ok," she confirmed. "I understand."

The pair fell silent as they cuddled closely together. There were a million things that needed to be said, but all of that could wait. Raine was simply enjoying being in Denny's arms.

****

Sometime during the day, Raine and Denny had fallen asleep. Raine woke up before Denny and decided to let her rest. As she got out of bed carefully, she immediately tried not to fall back over. As she caught sight of herself in the mirror, it dawned on her just how much damage she had taken; her body was covered in scars, the tip of one of her ears was torn, and someone's claw had marred her smile. After everything that had happened, she was a different woman. Not only that, but she was now the shapeshifter who had saved Denny's life. She was the protector of their little family.

In silence, Raine left the room and crept down the stairs. Each step hurt more than the last but she needed to know if the others were ok. All of their lives had been put at risk because of her.

She was overjoyed to realise that the house was noisy, happy and lively. She followed the sound through the twisting hallways and into the kitchen. The entire pack was crowded around the table and food was being passed around. There were a few faces missing, but she had expected it to be worse. Some of the weight that had been holding her down eased from her shoulders. Tears pricked her eyes as she looked at the people who had become her family.

Lucas smiled as he got up from the table and went to greet Raine. He too was scarred from the battle but it hadn't dented his morale.

"There you are!" he said. "We were wondering when Denny would finally let you out of bed. She was adamant that you needed to rest."

"She's certainly stubborn, isn't she?" Raine said, laughing a little as she moved to take a seat next to Shelly.

Shelly grabbed a spare plate and loaded it with food. She set it down in front of Raine before passing her a fork.

"She's a keeper," Shelly said. "Now eat. We need you to get better as fast as you can, so we can promote you."

"Promote me?"

"Yes," said Lucas. "What you've done for the pack is more than worthy of promotion. You took down more enemy shifters than I could count at the time. You're the one who figured out what was happening, and what we needed to do. You're the one that all of us owe our lives to."

Noticing Denny walk into the room, Raine hoped that she would be forgiven for having crept out of bed.

"I told you to rest," Denny said, half jokingly. "I see you. Don't think that we won't be having words about this later."

The shifters around the table laughed. Raine grinned as Denny took a seat next to her. She didn't seem out of place amongst the pack. In fact, it looked like she felt right at home.

"Back to the promotion news," Lucas said as he turned to Raine with a smile. "You are now the second-in-command.”

Raine nearly choked on her food as she looked at Lucas. There was no way that she could handle having that much power within the pack. It was too much and too soon. Her heart was beating rapidly in her chest and sweat was beading on her forehead.

“Stop looking as if he’s just given you the worst news of your life,” Shelly said as she lightly elbowed Raine. “This is a good thing and you aren’t alone. We’re in this together. That is, as long as you and Denny are willing to stay with the pack?”

Although Shelly was only trying to help, it did nothing to ease Raine’s concerns. It panicked her to wonder how she could possibly bring a human into the pack. Besides, she had never thought of herself as a leader before and more as a lone wolf – well, panther!

“I’m not going anywhere,” Denny whispered, putting her hand on Raine’s thigh and giving it a gentle squeeze.

Raine nodded and looked around the table. Whilst the pack had never been perfect or easy to live with, they were her family. She belonged with them and so did Denny. The life in front of them was becoming clear. It would be happy, and full of love and laughter.

"Together?" Raine asked.

"Forever," Denny said with a smile.

****